Among the Missing

Poems by
Cathy Bobb

Snake~Nation~Press
Founded 1989
110 West Force Street
Valdosta, Georgia 31601
www.snakenationpress.org

i

~:~

Snake Nation Press wishes to thank:
Barbara Passmore & The Price-Campbell Foundation
The Georgia Council for the Arts
Gloria & Wilby Coleman
Lowndes/Valdosta Arts Commission
Dean Poling & *The Valdosta Daily Times*
Blake Ellis
Our Subscribers

Snake Nation Press, the only independent literary press in south Georgia, publishes two Snake Nation Reviews, a book of poetry by a single author each year, and a book of fiction by a single author each year. Unsolicited submissions of fiction, essays, art, and poetry are welcome throughout the year but will not be returned unless a stamped, self-addressed envelope is included. We encourage simultaneous submissions.

Subscriptions
Individuals $30
Institutions $40
Foreign $40
Sample Copy $12 (includes shipping)

Published by Snake Nation Press
110 West Force Street
Valdosta, Georgia 31601

ISBN: 978-09863589-1-3

~:~

Among the Missing

Poems by
Cathy Bobb

*Snake Nation Press is a small non-profit press
dedicated to publishing literature
in all its myriad forms.*
110 West Force Street
Valdosta, Georgia 31601
www.snakenationpress.org

Acknowledgments

Spoon River Poetry Review, in which appeared "Cleaning House," "Coma," "Daughter," "In October," "Neanderthal," "Office Girl," "Shell," "Tender," "View From an Asylum," and "Visiting the Cemetery on All-Souls Eve."
Rock & Sling, for "Kingdom."
MotherVerse, for "Mirage" and "Visiting Our Daughter's Grave."

Art

Art on pages 63 and 77 by Jason Koltuniak.
Photographs on pages 31 and 69 by Vic Bobb.
Cover and back cover photographs by Vic Bobb.
Photograph on page 14 by Cathy Bobb.
Art on pages 2, 50, and 74 by Cathy Bobb.

~:~

for Vic

For Laura,
    Some see this only as a
book about struggle & tragedy
I have come to see it as a book
of love + how one can experience
both at the Same time.
                    Your friend,
                        Cath

~:~

Table of Contents

~:~

~:~

Shell

~:~

~:~

Shell

After eleven years the dresser
no longer serves a purpose.
It takes up space that could be
better used by the living.

I sit with the final drawer
on the floor beside me, deciding
what to keep. It takes time,
as I'm pulled by these things
as the moon pulls the tide.

These are the last things
cast up from the sea that
was my daughter's life.
Letters, earrings, keys,
snapshots of her friends
I had forgotten, a glove,
her hairbrush, drawings,
the shape of her mouth
pressed on slips of paper.
In the corner her watch.
I pick it up and hold it
to my ear.

~:~

Neanderthal

Digging with pick-axe and shovel,
lifting the flat stones by hand,
then trowel and brush
lest anything be overlooked or harmed,
science, with objective tenderness,
explores the shallow grave—
peels back the leather shroud,
measures the skull, femur,
photographs and numbers
the quiet curve of vertebrae,
accumulates figures, entering them
into cyber-vaults. Findings:
a Neanderthal, male, about twenty;
the tools with him suggesting
details of a brutish existence:
the clumsy knife and cup, scrapers,
an awl to pierce the animal hides he wore
laced with sinew.
It is not till later, in the lab,
that they would find
the microscopic remains
of love: pollen
from hundreds of flowers
that lined his grave
and covered his body.

~:~

Coma

You are naked except for the wires and tubes,
motionless except for breathing and pulse.
I turn you on your side and hold you there
so the nurse can place clean bedding under you.
You are lighter than I thought,
the way husks of moths
brushed from the window sill
surprise us with their lightness.
The nurse and I ease you to your back.
She arranges your gown across your body
and tucks it over your shoulders,
as though you were a paperdoll, and leaves.
I smooth your blankets
like pressing a flower in the pages of a book,
deciding for you
whether to put your hands
over or under the covers.

~:~

Sudden Darkness

Remember St. John the Revelator?
I never told you this
but I was always more horrified
by his blindness than his vision.
The morning you awoke to darkness,
I saw you sitting at the kitchen table,
waiting for dawn, waiting to tell us.

We never talked about what colors
people a sunrise, or mentioned
how the tail feathers curl on a mallard drake,
or the way the sun glints off his neck.
We never conversed on the
roundness of loaves
or the fullness of water.
Did you see these?

Are you just being strong for us,
or are you strong inside
where you sit in the dark?
Red chair, old boots,
candlelight, stars,
appleblossoms, hoar frost,
wash on the line, carp rising;
now I see.

~:~

Obituary

I wish I had known you:
the smell of your perfume, your laugh
(they say you laughed a lot).
I read your life in eight inches.
It left me aching for more.
To see you here among the others
makes me wonder
if I ever overlooked you
in the grocery store or park.
I am so busy and preoccupied
I rarely talk to strangers.
So I missed you in my life;
we could have drunk coffee
and talked of husbands and children.
What would you have surprised me with?
That you bucked bales behind a red truck;
that you once were a heretic;
that we both love Bach?
There will always be
an empty place in my life,
a missing puzzle piece
or book with a page torn out.
Stranger,
I believe the good things
they said about your life;
I believe you fought the good fight.
Courage is the word they used...
beloved, too.
One last look
before the newspaper goes in
with the wood
to warm me
this winter evening
without you.

~:~

Daughter

After he murdered you,
I couldn't remember

our last conversation,
I couldn't remember

the sound of your voice,
or your laugh.

I could not dream of you
for a year.

But I'd see you
in crowded places:

maybe the way
she wore her hair,

the angle of her chin,
the way another

moved her hand
or held her purse.

I could not look.
I could not look away.

~:~

Last Night

In the dream you're alive again, a child.
We are upstairs in the old house.
You are in your room. It is bare except
for a caged bird by the open window.

I cannot come into the room
and you cannot come out.
We sit on the floor at the doorway.
We are sad and we can't remember
what we needed to say to each other
but we talk anyway.

Suddenly I'm in the room
in front of the caged bird;
the bars are falling away
fast. I put my hands over
the holes to keep the bird in.
Finally my fingers are the only cage.
But I can't.
The bird flies out forever.
I cannot even see it.
I turn to you,
but you're gone.
I wake up.
And you are gone.

~:~

Mirage

They weep on buses,
in grocery stores and parks.
They are called barren,
young women
who find no relief in tears
but seek the pain of birth,
the tiny hand,
the eyes like his.

But I know the barrenness
of old women
whose children have died
or gone mad,
who sit and watch the fire go out.
They are like a desert.
Their memories betray them,
roads that wander
then disappear.

~:~

Eastern State Hospital

Insanity isn't at all what I expected.
It wasn't Lady Macbeth with guilt,
or Ophelia wild with grief.
It was the chemistry set in my brain,
misfiring neurons,
making sense of everything.
I learned God's middle name
and that walking on the black tiles
would lead me to hell,
or lunch: my choice.
They put me in someone else's clothes.
It was nice being that person,
except for the shoes.
If I put them on, I'd have to stay.
The voices announced to me I was the Virgin.
I told them I really wasn't up to it.
They said not to worry, they'd teach me,
So I started searching for the Savior.
I saw him in the visiting room
looking like my husband
but he left without me.
The princes of this world carry keys;
you notice things, like how
locking and unlocking a door
makes the same sound.

~ : ~

Guanajuato

It is worse than you thought,
this house for the dead.
Hung up like stringers of fish
for the world to see,
bodies dressed in death's best:
lace, taffeta, linen, and serge,
desiccated hollows,
skin stretched taut over bones,
mouths unhinged in wordless goodbyes.
Here are mothers and children,
fathers, aunts, grandmothers
upright, shoulder to shoulder,
lining the glass-cased walls.
You know you always wondered.
Here it is
unveiled
like a bride
before the kiss.

~:~

First Winter in Illinois

I went out without a coat
to feed the birds,
but stopped in awe;
whether God be merciful or not
my body knew this cold
would kill me
in minutes

I spread the seed
and with fingers already numb
put the suet in its cage
then ran inside
and locked the door.

~:~

Day After Christmas

The angels have gone back
to their heavenly homes.
The shepherds have returned
to fields and flocks.
The humble who came,
called to the stable by word of mouth,
have seen and gone home.
It is the second day of the incarnation;
the child who is God contents himself
at his mother's breast,
worthy and waiting for his Father's call
to engage Satan in the desert
far, far away from the sawdust
and tools of his earthly father.
For some this day after his birth
the world shines brighter than his star,
brighter than the Hand who made the eyes
that have not seen, not believed.

~:~

To A Friend Going First

for Don Wall

The flowers you picked for me
are letting go one by one.
Perhaps it is better
to throw a bouquet away
while it is fresh….
To love one day
and part the next:
it is not that love dies;
the hurt is when it doesn't.

Losing Sight

When I touch flowers
will I remember the colors
of geranium and phlox
and all the others?
Will pale yellow go first?
Then what will follow?
Will I be able to picture
you in your old faded jacket,
or that you are conducting
the best part of the music?
Will I lose how you
look at me when
what flames do to night
the passages of a day
the quiet stars?
Will I lose
all things that take flight?
Will darkness erase
the tired slope of your shoulders
when you come through the door;
the geography of your stoop
as you greet the dog.
Will I remember well enough
her prance,
the pink ball brought
with hopeful canter?
Or will my heart
see clearly then,
clearly enough
to let go
altogether?

Scarecrow

I see you at first
a staccato of motion
in my peripheral vision.
I hear you talking to the air,
arms conducting, hands punctuating
the tangle of your words.
The sea parts before you
as you tack down the sidewalk.
If I look into your eyes
will I be pulled into the vortex
of your internal landscape?
Is it a world without windows?
Will I be hunted by voices,
driven by delusions, no rest,
comfortless as you are?
You didn't choose this.
You can't stop long enough
to work, or dream or live in a house.
Your clothes peel away in tatters;
there is hunger in your face.
I look for the thread
that will tie you to us
living on the outside.
Did you once play Chopin?
Did you ever love?
Were you your mother's favorite?
Are you your Father's child?

~:~

In October

My husband came home
with six small, perfect apples for me,
picked from a tree
that grew in a wheat field
he hunted as a boy with his father.
He told me many times
of their late afternoon pilgrimages
before returning to car and home,
of the apples hard and sweet,
of knowing in their silence
that there were none better.
His father is frail now,
his hand working the remote
in the quest for something as good;
and when he speaks
in his voice I hear
the fierce and frightening
hunger of the old.

~:~

Demeter

I had a graceful young tree,
a Japanese maple,
that I carelessly let winter over
in its pot on the porch.
I feared that the root
holding its life
had frozen beyond redemption.

The snow was deep on the ground
when in early February
I peeled back a little bark on one branch
and was relieved to see the green life there,
as welcome as the haze of breath
on a mirror
or pulse
in the neck.

I knew the buds should swell next:
they were waiting for the sap
to rise and flourish them like wings
emerging from a chrysalis.

Way past spring,
well into June,
the buds still waited,
alive but unchanged,
like someone beneath the surface
holding her breath,

like waiting for the kiss
of a daughter
who leaves for the day
and never returns

~:~

First Day

This is a cold spring rain,
but it is the first day
without a fire in the woodstove
since we started burning in the fall,
on a day such as this.

~:~

Cleaning House

Progress.
Sorting out the drawers and shelves and closets—
how good to purge at fifty
those things I do not want at eighty:
directions to long-defunct appliances,
postcards from places I'll never go,
keys to what?
But the photo of one friend,
dead many years,
this one second frozen from his life:
my hand hesitates
then drops it into the trash.
What happens in the hour or so
before I retrieve it,
I am not sure.

~:~

Good Night

The robin announces the night,
the gathering in of what we see,
dusk subtracting the elements of our life.
The lilacs, white as love, persist.

~:~

A Far Country

~:~

When I Woke Up

When I woke up
my wrists were tied to the bed rails.
I lay there like a stone god or a chrysalis
that would open to a life of wings.
My covers lay smooth and undisturbed
like me. Being tied did not make me mad.
It gave me an excuse finally to do nothing.
I laughed. Far away I could make out
my legs and feet. I moved them because I could.

I did not wonder why I was in a hospital.
I knew it was a test. Everyone I had seen here
was a demon or an angel. No, really
a demon or an angel. The call button
was pinned to my blanket where I could reach it.
I pressed it because I could, wondering what
would show up.

                    A demon. Just my luck.
I told her I needed the bathroom. I tried to think
but could not. On the way one of my voices,
the one in charge, said to fall down and fight her off.
How they got there so fast…so many of them…
I fought them all and then the needle
and I was out.

When I woke up I was on a bare mattress
on the floor of a padded room. There really are such
places. I was not tied. It was quiet and dark.
The door, I knew, would be locked. I did not care.
Two of them came with another syringe of sleep.
Why not?…why not?

~:~

When I woke up I stretched and stood up.
It was quiet and dark. A small square of light,
the tiny window in the door drew me over.
I could see the nurses' station, bright
and decked out like a float in a parade
with flowers. Flowers for patients.
There were cards sticking out from between roses
or chrysanthemums or lilies. Cards from people.
For the first time I felt something. Sadness.
They were so beautiful, so good, the flowers.
They nodded to me, but none were mine. They were
from people who wanted their loved ones to return
to homes and families and work.
You could not leave this place
without flowers. None for me.
None for me.

~:~

Schizophrenia

My body is host to odd terrors
of jackals consuming me
from the inside of afternoon
shadows draping their length
across the meaning of another day
like this of times with friends
who apprehend the places missing
from my soul of paying with
incomprehensible fire for every
pleasure of each conversation
amputating me further from
the world of man.

Let us ride out into the country
and see if I can be found wandering there.

~:~

Occupation

A mated pair of Cooper's hawks
has nested in the pines
on the west side of our yard.
Moving down the food chain
has transformed the neighborhood:
the songbirds are silent,
the doves don't come to drink anymore,
and we've stopped feeding the quail.
Our dogs now bring in
the cast-off parts
of squirrels and songbirds
left to scavengers.

This morning I watched one of the raptors
on the top branch of a bull pine
skillfully stripping off
the plumage of its kill,
watched as the feathers took their last flight,
the wind carrying them like black snow.

~:~

Hunger

It moves the hawk to our yard in deep winter,
calls coyotes down from the hills.
In February the deer are tame with hunger,
the cub finds the teat of his sleeping mother,
the winter sleepers rise with it.
It is the song of the woods and hedgerows.
It wakes the moth at sundown
and raises the bat from her stupor.
It is the root seeking the soil,
the mosquito the heart's blood.
It keeps us alive—
Only we who fell from grace,
only we hunger
for unnecessary things.

~:~

Yellow Lilies

My husband gave me a bouquet of large yellow lilies,
emblematic and full of hope.
It is hailing and cold, the house is in disarray.
He has taken over his father's slippers. I'm not sure why.
The clothes we gave his dad in his last months
were not worn after he tried them on.
They hung loosely on what was left.
We all exclaimed how nice he looked,
then he would take them off and fold them back into the boxes
without comment. Papa could never remember
the name of the disease that was killing him.
In such confusions we live and die.

When Christmas came, he wanted nothing.
"I should not be here," was his explanation.
He stayed on until July Fourth. It was not his choice,
but some habit of breath and heart.

~:~

Reading the Dead

There they are again, back for a last word,
Section C, somewhere between
the softball scores and Apartments, Unfurnished.
Some look out at us from youthful faces,
though they left us old;
others meet our gaze with eyes
to whom dying had become a way of life,
brave looks and their last birthday smiles.

Nice suit…he was probably surprised
to wake up dead and out of a job.
This one, not in focus, couldn't hold still
long enough to get a decent picture.
Cap on backwards...he has had his last drink.
I cannot look at the babies long,
or the young; perhaps it was the hard frost
that killed them with the marigolds.

They are the dead and this is their curtain call.
They give me pause,
like this one, my age,
who did so much with her life.
Mine will never measure up:
she gave herself away;
my little hoarded life
will probably net me
an inch, maybe two.
And there is one other thing to envy:
everyone here knows the truth now,
all their questions answered
in the great wave
that carried them over.

~:~

Hating the Russians

It was our duty to hate them.
My sailor father hated them,
but hoped there would not be another war.

My pacifist mother would stand weeping
by my crib in DC when we lived
in the circle called Ground Zero.
She hated them in advance for killing me.
She hated them for not loving,
not ending all war with the power they had.

We did not hate them for what they did
to Poland, the Czechs, Lithuania, and the rest,
but we should have.

Me? I did not hate them
for time spent, hands behind my head,
curled in a ball in the clothes closet at school,
waiting for the all-clear siren;

I did not hate them
for making Math and Science harder,
though I did feel put upon;

I did not hate them
when Khruschev said
that they would bury me.

The night hatred for them
finally consumed me was when
they sent Laika into space
with no plan to retrieve her.

~:~

Act IV

As I grow older, my props
have multiplied exponentially.
Things seem to define the plot
rather than the plot, things.
I'm now possessed of cars, a house, tables,
beds, books, cooking pots;
I mean, I even have knickknacks,
something I swore I'd never be caught dead owning.
Which is the trouble,
being caught dead, I mean.
Weren't all these things
supposed to hold off the inevitable?
In the beginning, I'm sure
it said that somewhere.
Now toward the end
why do I have to see that everything,
every
single
thing,
is going to belong to
someone else some day.
It takes all the fun out of shopping
to know I'm just renting.

~:~

The Doll

When I was a child I would stand close
and watch her sew.
I could feel the hum of the sewing machine
in my chest and fingers as she made my clothes.
My mother's hands moved so quickly,
like a bird getting used to its cage.

Time and love had moved me
to a husband and children
when she sent me the gift, a doll.
I pictured how she had laid out
Grandma's wedding gown and
cut into it, making pieces for its dress,
the fabric so light and soft
I could barely feel it with my fingers.
I saw her square hands gathering
the tucks and fastening them
with a satin sash and a tiny velvet flower.
I felt the thread tightening down
the seed pearls on the bodice,
her needle and thimble
ticking as she worked.

She visited me in her seventy-fifth winter.
We were folding laundry together
when she asked me
where I got the doll.

~:~

View from an Asylum

Streams of the unquiet,
like dazed fish
in a too-small tank
pace through the thick air
down the hall, around
and back again, again
we pass the only picture in here.
It is a turbulent purple and yellow sunset
that covers the wall at the end of our ward.
I stand before it often,
for long periods of time,
my back to the meshed windows facing west
that offer me the unavailable sun.

~:~

It's A Girl Thing

His lover before me
was twenty-three the last time
we saw her weeping
beautifully on his porch.

He and I have grown old together.
Our love is strong...
yet she glides into my thoughts
—now and then—
I hope not into his.

Ah...but to ask
could plant a seed.
I realize somewhere
like us, she's sixty-one.
I want to pull her
weedy young body
out of our past
and into oblivion,

but first I want to know:
would he reject the girl she was
for the woman I am?

The lovers we leave
stay forever young.
Damn.

~ : ~

The Weight of Nothing

The tracks look like signatures
scrawled across the hillsides
where combines and farm trucks are harvesting wheat.
Some of the stubble has already been put to plow.
It is the end of a season
gone by too fast for me;
there should have been flowers;
there should have been efforts made.
I slept in my clothes for days the same
clothes waking and sleeping;
my hands lay fallow,
my back unbent.
If no crops are planted
the earth still produces weeds.
I envy her.

~:~

Mother, earth

At seventy-nine
she still plants her garden;
she personally escorts spring in,
celebrates the new green,
digging like a terrier for the joy;
taking the elements
of water, soil, and sun;
she sees the flower in the seedling.
She finds redemption in the earth,
a gratitude for seasons,
withholding nothing from her time;
she gives wholly to what is fleeting.

~:~

Room to Room

It happens to women over eighty:
this tendency to carry one's purse
from room to room, carefully
using both birdlike hands
in case one forgets. They look
like little girls playing dress-up
in too-big clothes, with handbags,
those grown-up things held tightly.
Inside: her medicine, address book,
a coinpurse that was his,
photographs of someone's children,
magnifying glass, lipstick,
nail file, comb, powder, handkerchief,
checkbook, and wallet with plastic cards
to pay for tomorrow if it comes.
She is ready to go, either way.

~:~

Visiting Our Daughter's Grave on All Souls' Eve

Feeling our way up the familiar rise,
we navigate by a single votive,
one of a thousand fragile lights.
It keeps watch as silent as the vacant trees,
holding a vigil more transient than our own.
The flame draws from the night bronze and granite,
and her name wavering like a pulse,
colder to my touch than the frosted
grass and leaves curled inward.
I cannot see the others finding their way
among the candles, only the absence
of flames as they pass.

~:~

Home Before Dark

for Jane Kenyon

Here nothing is planted on purpose anymore;
her daffodils and violets come up like afterthoughts…
the wheat encroaches on the yard
as lilacs die and stumps are pulled.
The pine's tired branches rest
on what is left of the kitchen porch;
between its broken spindles
a spider's precise home glistens.
Dressed in warped boards and rust,
the house leans into itself.
Wasps patrol under the eaves;
field mice rule the pantry;
along her fragile spine blackbirds
are gathering for winter.
In the chill of late afternoon
when shadows lie long across the fields,
under the threshhold
the cricket ceases its song.

~:~

Father-in-Law

My father-in-law was six feet tall.
At the end he weighed 94 pounds
He just wore out,
couldn't eat.
Those last months I realized
how much I liked and respected him,
how much I appreciated his stories
of his boyhood, courtship, and the war;
of the miles of fencerows he hunted
with his son and dogs;
of the goodness of his daughter's laughter.
Listening was all he needed from me.
He loved his wife with the simplicity of a child;
his praise for her would come often with tears.
This skeletal man always would say
how lucky he was...even at the end...
especially at the end.
The night he was so cold
he couldn't sleep, my husband
lay down beside him
and held him in his arms
until the old man closed his eyes.
The small box on the floor
by my husband's desk
is said to contain his father's remains.
I don't think so.

Portion

My husband is alone standing in his mother's kitchen
dividing the ashes of his father into smaller boxes.
They are labeled with the same tape and marker
his mother uses for canning.
Each portion is for a place he was rooted to:
the house in Mitchell that contained his childhood,
and Kenny's where he taught his son to hunt.
There is one for Chapman Lake where he caught
silvery trout perfect in the morning's light.
There are more. I can feel the care my husband
is using to measure and pour what we will sow
to the wind and earth, what we knew of him
with our eyes, ears, hands.
His mother sits on the couch playing with the puppy,
listening to a recording of her husband's voice
commenting on Benny Goodman's
"Stomping at the Savoy".
Big band music follows, threading through the house,
then Papa's voice again.
Three last containers will be kept by us,
something he wouldn't have expected
but each of us needed.
My mother-in-law asks my husband
if he is all right—
he answers, yes.
I listen from the dining room
as he washes his hands
and turns out the light.
We are the only sacrament Papa wanted.

~:~

Rival

After we made love
but before we slept,
I lazily embraced him.
My fingertips touched his side lightly
and discovered a lump
just below the rib Adam gave.
Here was a rival
who is either benign or not.

On such a delicate fulcrum
our world is balanced.
We've always known
we would be banished from the garden.
We just do not know when.

~:~

Normal

I appear to be standing
in line at the grocery store
like the woman in front of me
the woman behind
no one knows
every one knows
I'm wearing my sane face
the one I keep in my purse
how it was before
I cannot remember
I always remember
the heavy door shut
locked with two keys
no use to even try it
I keep trying

~:~

Intersection

He was standing on the bow of the concrete median,
a small black figure of misery.
The dark morning poured cold rain,
traffic lights trailed long red,
amber, and green ribbons on the wet asphalt.
I was in a hurry driving south when I saw him.
He stood mute, his wings hunched,
beak pointing toward the sky.

He was still and wounded,
Cars kept splashing through the gritty puddles,
water mixed with oil and sand coated his feathers.
The traffic light pushed the cars along.
I was caught in their stream,
but my heart remained with the crow.

I turned around at the park and headed back to rescue him,
if not from death, from the travesty of how and where.
I searched through the pulse of the wiper blades;
The median was vacant. I hoped for a moment,
then saw him not far from where he had stood,
lying like a stone in the gutter.
We had met at the fulcrum of life and death,
no help for either of us, he more stoic than I.

~:~

Prescription

As it comes time
I can feel the presence of the other
making a pass
the shark's first inquiry
before blood.
If I wait I begin to lose
the solidity of sight,
skittering movement
in the dimmer corners of the room
manifests creatures craving the light;
hesitation means the figure stands before me
pressing its face to my face,
breast to breast,
molecular violation;
within the droning of the fan
a multitude of voices sing,
chanting too softly for me
to catch the words.
If I delay, they will prophesy
in an oratorio of despair and destiny,
choruses not easily forgotten;
If I am late, grimacing faces
in the grain of table and wall,
or the meaningful gesture of the towel
draped over a chair
announce the quickening
of the inanimate.
Take one tablet three times daily
as prescribed.
I live in your world
only by invitation.

~:~

Drift

Lying in your arms,
your body curved around my back,
I feel your breathing,
the benediction of your hand
lightly touching my head,
the tide of sleep taking you first.

~:~

Left

~:~

Brief

I expect your hand reaching for the plate.
I see the book you were reading;
you've probably finished it by now.
I fix enough for four. I expect you're sleeping in.
I find the perfect present for you. It must be you
at the door. These are the briefest of times,
fragile as a last breath, the final remnants
of everyday peace, the persistence of expectation,
the habits of love—each uprooted in turn,
strewn over the landscape of grief.

~:~

Left

Your lover came today to tell us
how hard the last months have been.
That he almost took his own life
after yours was taken.

When summer brought
the climbing rose to bloom
with hundreds of flowers
overflowing his porch,

he cut down all the blossoms:
all of them. He pulled the armloads
out of his car, unaware of the blood,
and covered your grave.

~:~

For The Man In The Plastic Bag

I met a man once in Portland.
I never knew his name,
it was on a tag
tied to his toe.
I didn't get up to look.

They parked his gurney in front of me
and left him there.
I was sitting on a bench
waiting for the lab to draw my blood
in the hospital's cavernous basement.

Life was in me:
pregnant with my first,
and in front of me lay the dead man
naked in a clear plastic bag.
Unembarrassed and unashamed,
I stared, we were alone.

He looked barely fifty,
a handsome man with short grey
and silver hair, clean shaven.
He had a large chest,
long slender legs.
Death had left no mark.
He didn't even look sick,
but like he might open his eyes and speak.

~:~

He was a person I would never know,
an orphan out of time.
For some he was a task now
an object to be removed,
even as some would think
Benjamin in my womb a thing,

For me, Ben and he
are linked inextricably
like inhaling and exhaling,
And I loved the dead man:
without history,
without meaning to.
I watched him
tenderly,
like a newborn
in his crib.

~:~

Embrace

for the young woman lost off
Dominical Beach, Costa Rica, August 2008

She knew the sea,
but not the river under the sea.
The riptide gathered her beyond her skill—
and with the failing of her strength
came knowledge that she would never
feel the earth against her feet,
nor her mother's kiss again.
The waves crowned her with foaming veil;
she was the bride of death and knew it.
And then the sea was in her
consummating a life she could not recall
and she forgot the name that christening drops
had laid upon her head some twenty years before.

~:~

Fall

The flickers are spending
more time in the attic.
Leaves fill the gutters.
Squirrels are hoarding somewhere
between the walls.
I should do something
but life being what it is
it will soon enough be
someone else's problem.

~:~

Unstitched

His heart lay mysterious
and still somewhere beneath
the tie I gave him
for his last birthday.

The disease
in its suicidal victory
had fallen perversely
benign among the ruins.

As I stepped closer
I saw a gash on his forehead,
bloodless, open as a mouth,
wordless before me.

It struck me
it would scar
if not stitched.

Life has a habit
of thinking about wounds.
Death doesn't give a damn.

It was the end
of the last conversation
we never had.

~:~

Scars

They are the sign of something taken
from the earth, the body, the heart:
the hardened map of pain,
redemption's price.

~:~

Liebestod

The best summer nights in the midwest
cool the soft moist air
into swirling mists.

Fireflies at dusk rise from the sweet grass
of lawns or clearings in the small
brushy stands of woods.

They rise and fall near the earth to be caught
in our hands and released or gathered
into canning jar lanterns.

When the old house was asleep I would rise naked,
my feet on the smooth
warm floorboards;

Through the opening in the lace curtains
I would watch the cold streetlight
with its pulsating halo of insects.

There were hordes of moths and others dancing
in frenzied flight as the light demanded
until death overtook them:

Ravenous bats and nighthawks leaving trails of nothing.
My young husband and I on our nightly walks found
hundreds of wings under these lights;

wings of luna moths, gallinippers, and mayflies,
dark wings and pale, a puzzle never
to be assembled.

~:~

It was our way to walk the small town end to end,
cornfields to railroad tracks. People opened
up their houses to let them breathe.

We could see inside, the grey flickering light
of their TVs, the generations of pictures
on their walls.

We watched fat men in boxers and thin sleeveless
undershirts, lying on couches
with doilies. We'd see

kids' rooms with bunkbeds and clothes draped everywhere,
wives closing cupboard doors sweating
from family work,

teenagers and old couples sitting on porches
on half discarded furniture, watching
the heat lightning.

We'd walk by invalids' houses sealed tightly. What we
could glimpse through the crack in the shades
gave us oxygen cannisters and wheelchairs,

and dying people with hair like first feathers on baby birds.
We'd walk faster, circling around back of our own house,
to the overgrown alley.

Surrounded by pokeweed, Viginia creeper, and hemlock,
full of the sounds of frogs and crickets,
the sound of our breathing

~:~

~:~

Kingdom

An hour before dawn, a birth in blood,
a prison of thorns, within the twisted tangle
the thrush prepares her song, a sacrifice of praise,
her purest offering.

The river of travail rises from the root
of the storm, to vine and branch,
repairs the peace that was lost,
prepares the fruit, without season.

Yet in the darkness dividing all from all,
such longing for the light, each creature
searches for her own, prepares the feast
of straw instead of meat. The foxes and
the rabbits will share their dens,
this laying down a humble gift for
what could not come
will come.

Rich corruption for the worm
feasting on our sorrows. The lowly despot
Lord of the night, King of all flesh, he is
ruler death without death. What can depose
what tears nor might cannot,
Dawn is preparing

A vision of the rose imbues the bee
born this morning with hope, though he's
never seen a flower, twined in the earth, tendrils
white and slow curl beneath last fall's leaves preparing.

The lamb and the lion wake this dawn to find they are
the same flesh and the same blood,
The last vestige of the longest night
retreats, cringing, from the pale sunrise
and the grate of the rolled back stone.

~:~

Knowing

The weight of my coat
when the lost keys
are in the pocket.

That there's enough flour.

The dog's smile
when she has found
something to roll in.

That the chair will fit
through the door somehow
when we've already failed twice.

When there's enough gas
to get me there.

That it will take another stamp.

That the hair on his jacket
is mine.

The feel of the last stair
in the dark.

~:~

Winter Nap

From her place by the fire
to my cold winter bed
my terrier has brought with her
the warmth of the woodstove.
More constant than a shadow,
she settles cupped
at the back of my knees
as we curl into sleep.
Such friends light
the darkness of the day.

~:~

Office Girl

She takes off her sweater
and folds it over the back
of the bench and sits down.
For 25 minutes she is her own.
She opens the bag and pulls out
a foldover sandwich
and a small bunch of grapes.
She unbuttons just the top button
and leans back,
no book, no sunglasses.
Shoes and socks come off and she explores
the grass with her toes like a child.
Around her the air is sweet with blossoming trees,
the bees in them worshipping
without prayer, without pause.
The sun warms her face; she closes her eyes.
I watch her, urging her from my desk inside
not to return to hers.
I wish her petals on naked skin
and belonging to no one.

~:~

Introduction

The whisper of leaves dropping
on a windless autumn day,
swooshing knee-deep through them,
the crackle of the fireplace at home,
the farewell songs of migrating birds and weary crickets.
A leaf caught in the spider's last web
is trembling in the breath of fall.

Snow falling with a holy quiet,
the private exchange of our own breathing
loud under wintry layers,
the squeak of boots in snow as we walk to get the mail,
the heavy crunch of making the biggest snowball ever,
chatter of the birds who stayed.
Wind shearing through the frozen branches
and up under the eaves in the early dark
gathers us into the sounds of home.

The welcomed gurgle of water
out from under the snow in sparkling rivulets,
the high tinkling of icicles dripping,
the first returning robin singing
to himself for the joy of it,
the bee in the blossom buzzing
and busy in the center of the world.
The outside-in sound of screen doors closing
and windows opening,

The ringing of ice in the glass when we drink,
from high in the trees cicadas calling each to the other,
the growl of gravel under bike tires,
the treble pitched delight of children
playing in water,
the dry voices of grasshoppers

~:~

keeping ahead of us in the weeds,
the rush and hush of wind in the wheat,
the melody of your parents singing to you
since before you were born.
Sing, little one
This is the song.
This is the symphony.

For Liam Webster, age One Day

Wasp

In his dusty velvet jacket
the old man of the windowsill
rises again on battered wings
to the lying glass.
The sound of his efforts
is quieter than before.
He has stopped beating into the pane,
this puzzlement, this curse
he has spent the afternoon
trying to escape.
As he falls to the sill again
I watch him, his body heavy, exhausted,
a comma of weariness,
his head low in defeat.
I expect to see him next on his back
staring with compound vision
at a thousand suns,
but a strong breeze
has blown open the door
beside my desk,
its cool river of air giving him direction.
He turns and with a burst of miraculous strength
rises upon its familiar joy
through the doorway and up
beyond my sight.
A silent benediction
stirs my dark heart:
this afternoon's harbinger of death
has gained our reprieve.

~:~

When I Contemplate Going Blind

It is different now when I close
my eyes to sleep.
I lie there measuring the length
and breadth of darkness,
the weight of it on my soul.
My eyes will not stay shut
and like a swimmer from the deep
coming up for air with burning lungs,
I breathe in with gratitude
the glowing clock face,
the lace curtains etched with moonlight,
the outline of my sleeping husband,
and tread the water of my night.
I'm told it will come slowly at first,
that I will adjust in time.
I'm told that when this evening comes
I will still dream with sight—
see the seasons change
with my unconscious whim;
that my dreams will take me back
to color, form, and shape.
Then, I will know no darkness
darker than when I wake.

~:~

Requiem For A Summer Evening

From the porch at dusk
I see the red sun in the arms of the pine,
the rocky hills dressed in long shadows.
I breathe in the silhouettes
of trees cast upon the open faultless sky.

Above the river glides
the circular descending flight
of geese setting down for the night,
the vacant air of the clearing
suddenly alive with bats,
raveners of day.

You've brought me a cold glass of water
without me asking, and join me
as color leaves the sky.
Then darkness, like surrender,
lies over us.
We watch the moths;
their erratic wings are tiny flames
in the glow from the window.
My hand finds yours.
My evening is full of small sorrows.

To hold on with fear to fragile gifts
is to have lost them already.

~:~

Husband

When I first lost my mind,
you could have left too.
It never occurred to you.
When the medicine took me
away in milligrams,
you sheltered me.

I came back in inches over years
while the life you were planning
you lost in miles.
You gracefully relinquished it.

You cherished, honored and cheered me.
You never faltered,
and although you drew maps for me,
you never said I was lost.

You welcomed me with
your eyes, words,
body, heart;
you even love
the ghost I sometimes am
and have not grown bitter
waiting for the dead
to rise again.

~:~

Tender

We are in the car in between
nowhere in particular.
You who never tire
at the newness of familiar things
point out, just before we arrive,
every pond where there might be
some redwings,
or the low spot in the swale
greener than the rest,
the place the barn
isn't anymore,
the sandy bend where
the heron might stand.
You do this for me,
who has lived inward
for so long
that I have missed
too often
the ordinary repeated beauties
of this road we're on.

~:~

Heart

I lie with my head resting
just to the left of the scar
that saved your life.
I hear inside you
what is steady again.

When we were young
I could not bear to lie
with my head on your chest.
There were four of us then:
you, me, love, fear.

Today, for the joy of it,
I lie with my ear over your heart.
I cannot explain this mystery of age.
I am aware that death has touched
your heel and cast you back,
and that Now is another grace.

~:~

Poet's Statement

My husband, two children, and I had been living in Charleston, Illinois, for nearly nine years. Everything was going along in a fairly normal fashion when at age 39 I began to hear voices. I saw grimacing faces in the leaves of the tree across the street and in the grain of our wooden floors and in the wrinkles of clothes draped over a chair. I began to feel powerful dread and a burning sensation on my skin. I was slipping into another place: the world of schizophrenia.

After two short stays in psychiatric units and months of intense suffering, I was finally diagnosed and put on medication that I take daily to control symptoms. The medicine allows me to live a blessedly "normal" life. In 1986 we moved to Spokane, Washington, where our 17 year old son developed the same disease...but medication has proved much less effective for Ben, and he is largely disabled by his fears and delusions. In 1993, our 20 year old daughter, Mary, was murdered by a co-worker. I have watched over the past twenty years as my mother-in-law bravely fights macular degeneration and is now almost totally blind. I learned a few years ago that I have the precursor to that same condition. I am not so brave.

I came to write poetry in 2000 when I quit my job as a retail clerk and took a poetry writing workshop from Laurie Lamon at Whitworth University. She opened the door and turned on the light. Poems poured out of the place in me that had had no voice before. I found myself writing about a variety of things, including many facets of death. I am not a ghoul. We all live in death's neighborhood; quite a few of my poems are for honoring the dead and for not letting them go just yet.

There is a poem feeling I get when I'm going to write. A phrase or something I've seen or something I've read or a sudden insight comes to me, and it persists. When I actually sit down to write, I put down on paper everything that comes into my head without weighing it. Then,

~:~

I shape and clarify meaning and sound by crossing things out as the poem emerges. New lines occur to me as I make revision after revision. Usually the end of the poem comes as a total surprise to me. It comes like an answer to an unspoken question from somewhere else and fits into place like the keystone of an arch.

I love the whole process of writing. It is one of my deepest pleasures. Also, I find I enjoy doing readings. As the audience responds to my works, and with the risk-taking of speaking candidly with them, we create a gratifyingly intimate atmosphere.

My husband, Vic, once said that Art is a conduit both from and to the truth. I believe that truth is what actually is. When I was coming out of the delusions and unreality of schizophrenia, where all is false, I developed a love affair with reality. I believe that truth is a real and objective fact, however imperfect, fallible, or partial our perception of it might be. I believe that when we encounter truth in art, at a deep level a chord of recognition is struck in us. I want my poems to be that kind of art.

As I was discovering how deeply I love reality, because of the horrors of the untruth that is schizophrenia, I learned that I need to live in the truth. I found I was not particular that I live in just the pleasant realities. I embraced the difficult negative realities as well. Above all, during the time I was so profoundly ill, I found that the one thing that never wavered was God. I could trust Him to be Himself when other pillars claiming to be true crumbled under the weight of my disease. He was and is my Rock.

- Cathy Bobb

~:~

Among the Missing by Cathy Bobb
is the winner of the 2014
Violet Reed Haas Prize for Poetry
Judge: Snake Nation Press Editors

Previous Winners:

Penelope Scambly Schott for *The Perfect Mother*
Judge: Van K. Brock

Barbara Goldberg for *Marvelous Pursuits*
Judge: David Kirby

Seaborn Jones for *Lost Keys*
Judge: Robert Earl Price

Judith Hemschemeyer for *Certain Animals*
Judge: Judson Mitchum

Tania Rochelle for *Karaoke Funeral*
Judge: Marty Williams

Irene Willis for *At The Fortune Cafe*
Judge: Tania Rochelle

Lisa Zimmerman for *How The Garden Looks From Here*
Judge: Rick Campbell

Lana Hechtman Ayers for *Dance From Inside My Bones*
Judge: Irene Willis

Starkey Flythe for *The Futile Lesson of Glue*
Judge: John Guzlowski

Judith Hemschemeyer for *How Love Lives*
Judge: Starkey Flythe

Nagueyalti Warren for *Braided Memory*
Judge: Judith Hemschemeyer

George Young for *The Astronomer's Pearl*
Judge: Snake Nation Press Editors

Kevin Brown for *A Lexicon of Lost Words*
Judge: Snake Nation Press Editors